Once upon a time, a princess was born in a *faraway* land. The king and queen were so happy.

"Let's have a party," said the king.

"Yes!" said the queen. "We will *invite* three *fairy* **godmothers**."

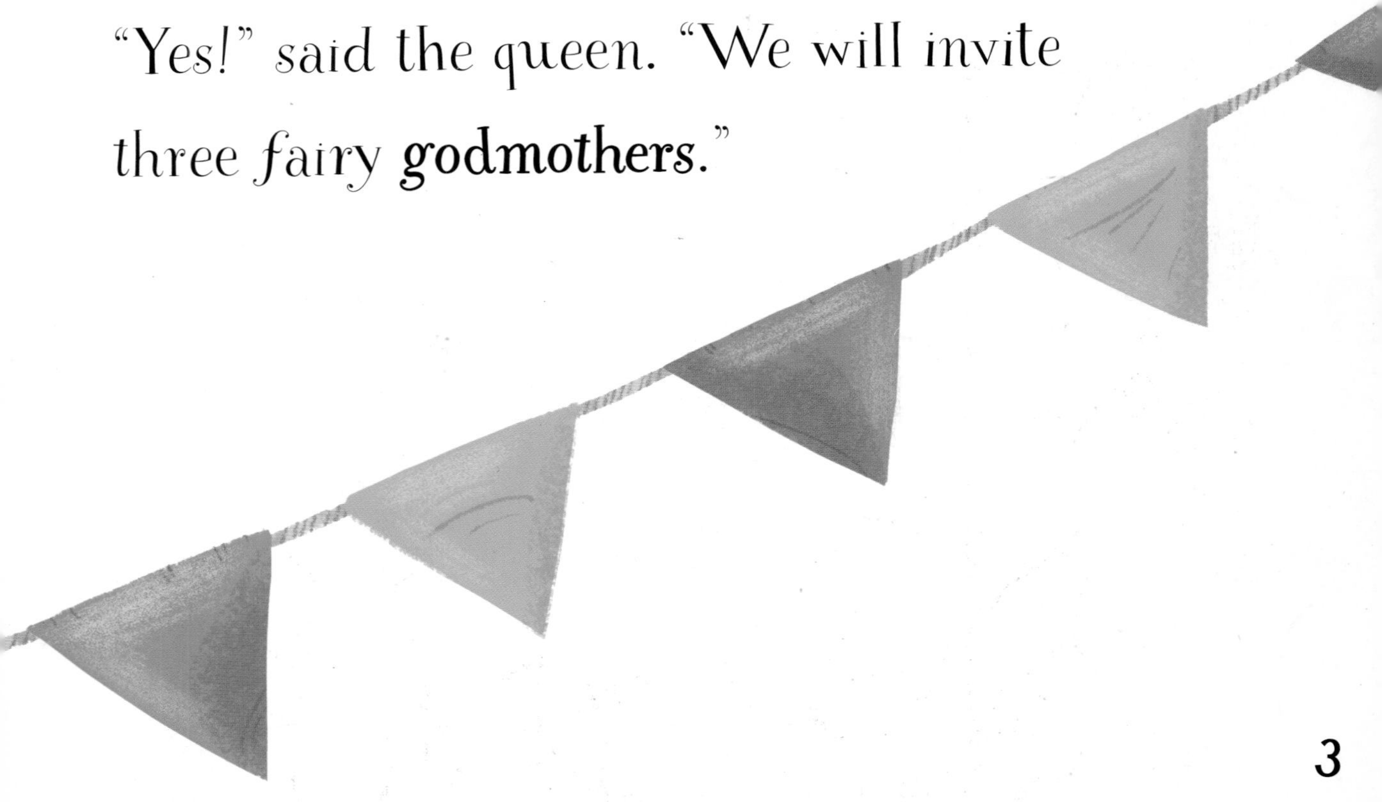

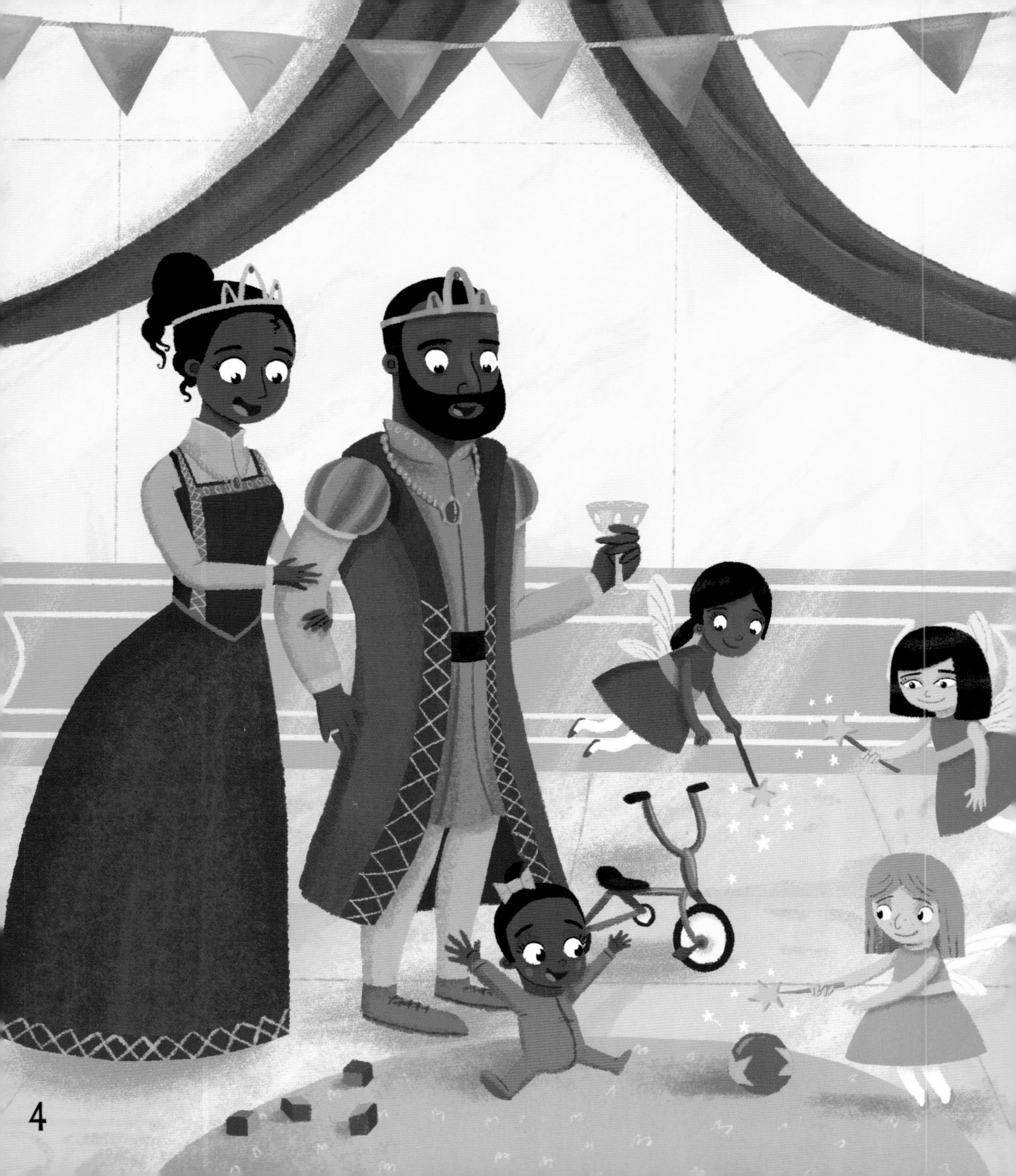

FAIRY TALE MIX-UPS

The Frog Prince
Saves
Sleeping Beauty

written by Charlotte Guillain
illustrated by Dan Widdowson

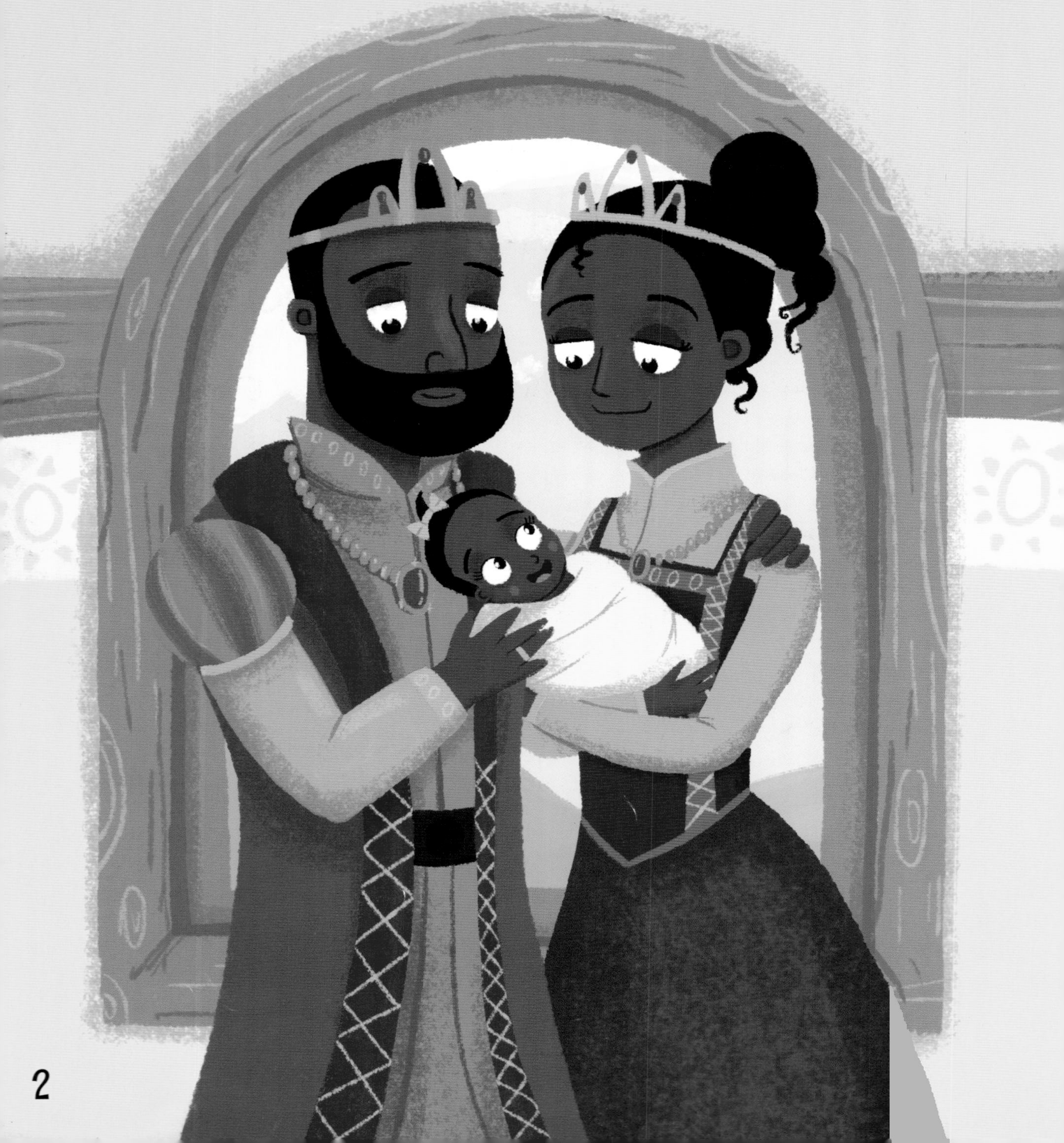

The day of the party arrived. The *fairy* **godmothers** brought their magic wands.

SHAZAM! A sparkly tricycle appeared.

SHAZAM! There was a shiny ball.

But just as the third *fairy* godmother waved her wand, the doors flew open.

"What's happening?" cried the king.

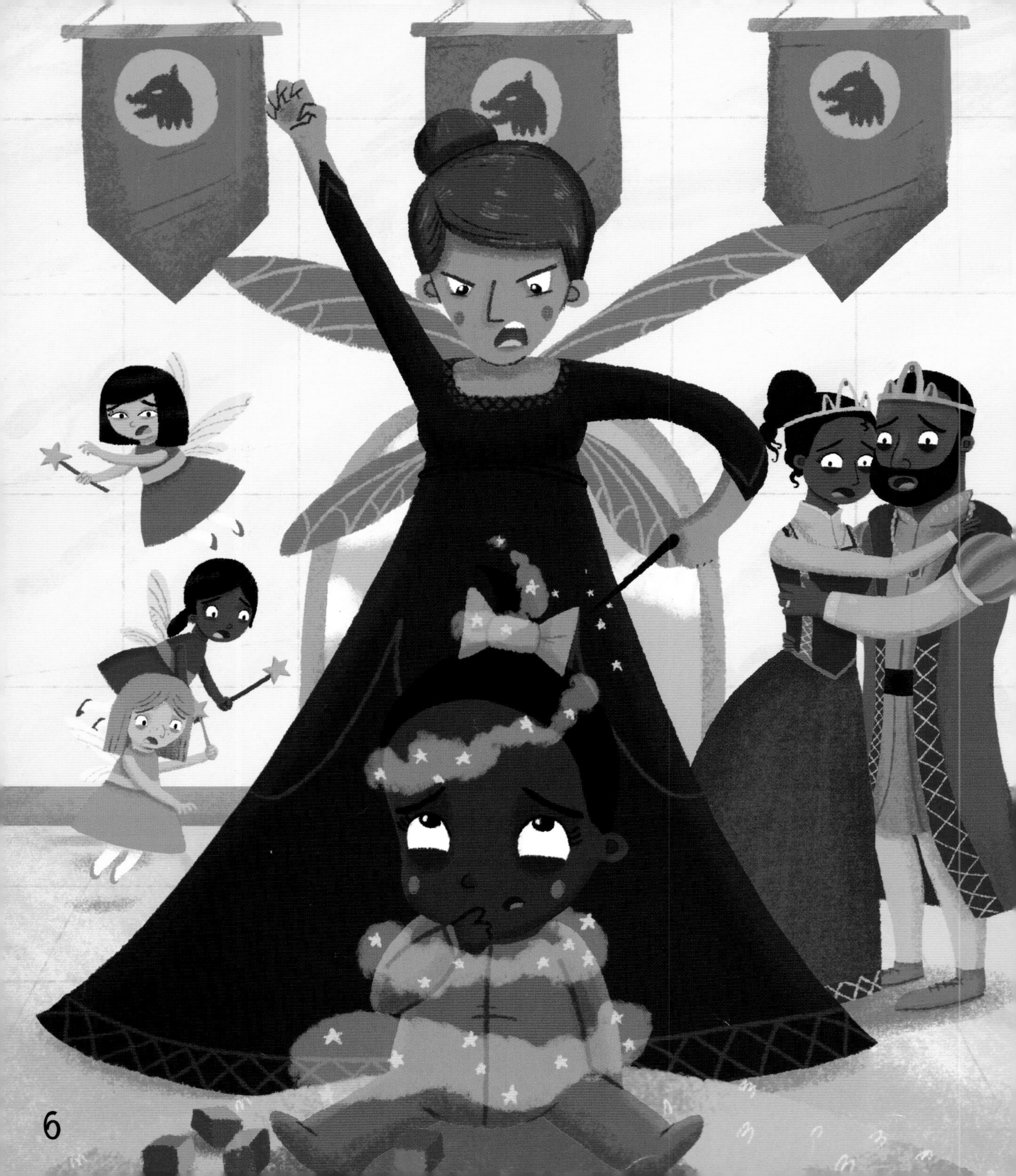

A wicked fairy flew into the room.

"You didn't invite me," she **cackled**. Everyone shivered with fear.

"My present for the princess is a **curse**," said the wicked fairy. "If the princess pricks her finger before she is ten years old, she will die."

SHAZAM!

Everyone **gasped**. The wicked fairy vanished.

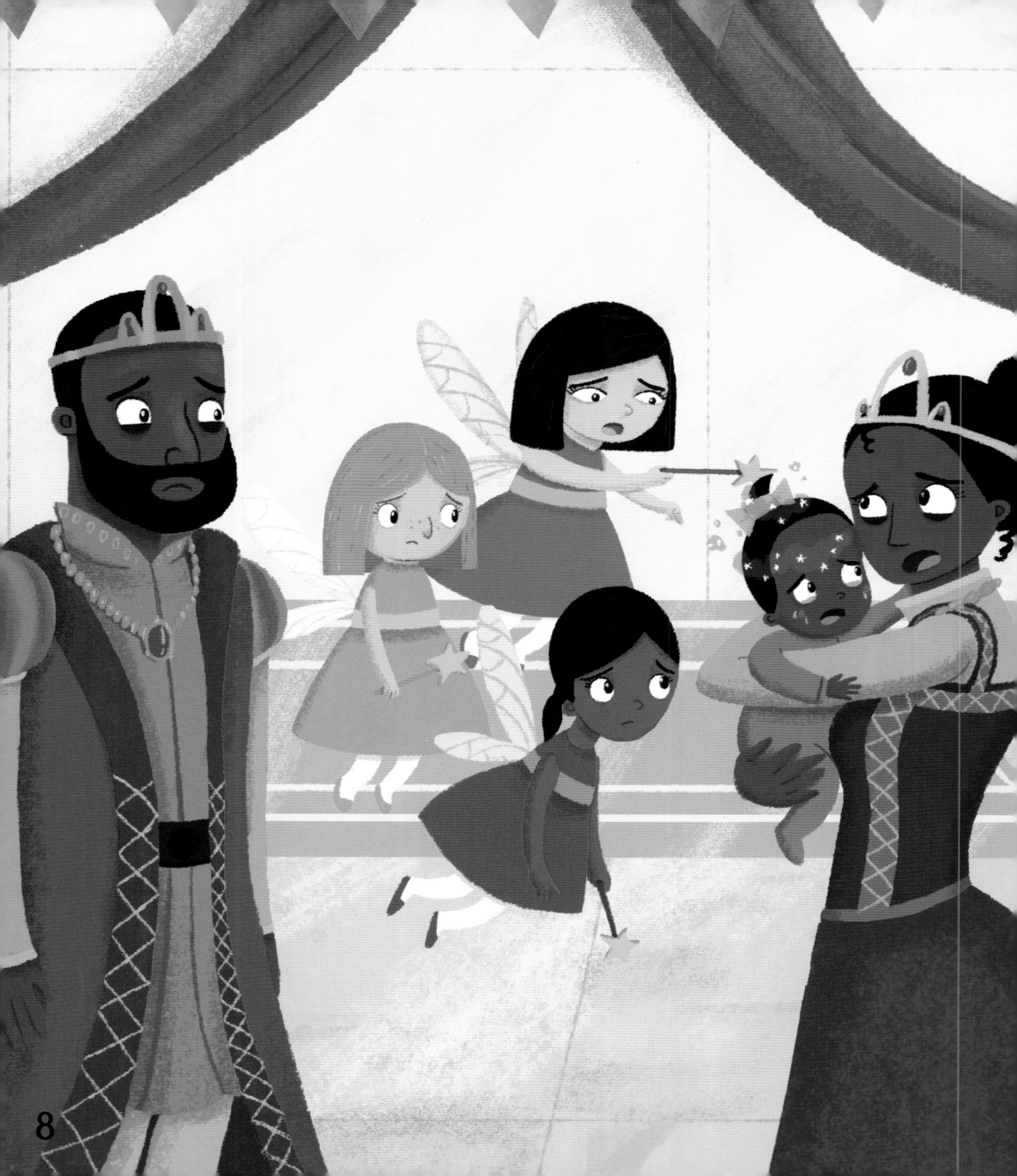

"Help us, please!" the king and queen begged the fairy **godmothers**.

"I can't stop the **curse**," said the third fairy godmother. "But I can change it. If the princess pricks her finger, she will not die. She will just sleep until she is kissed by a prince."

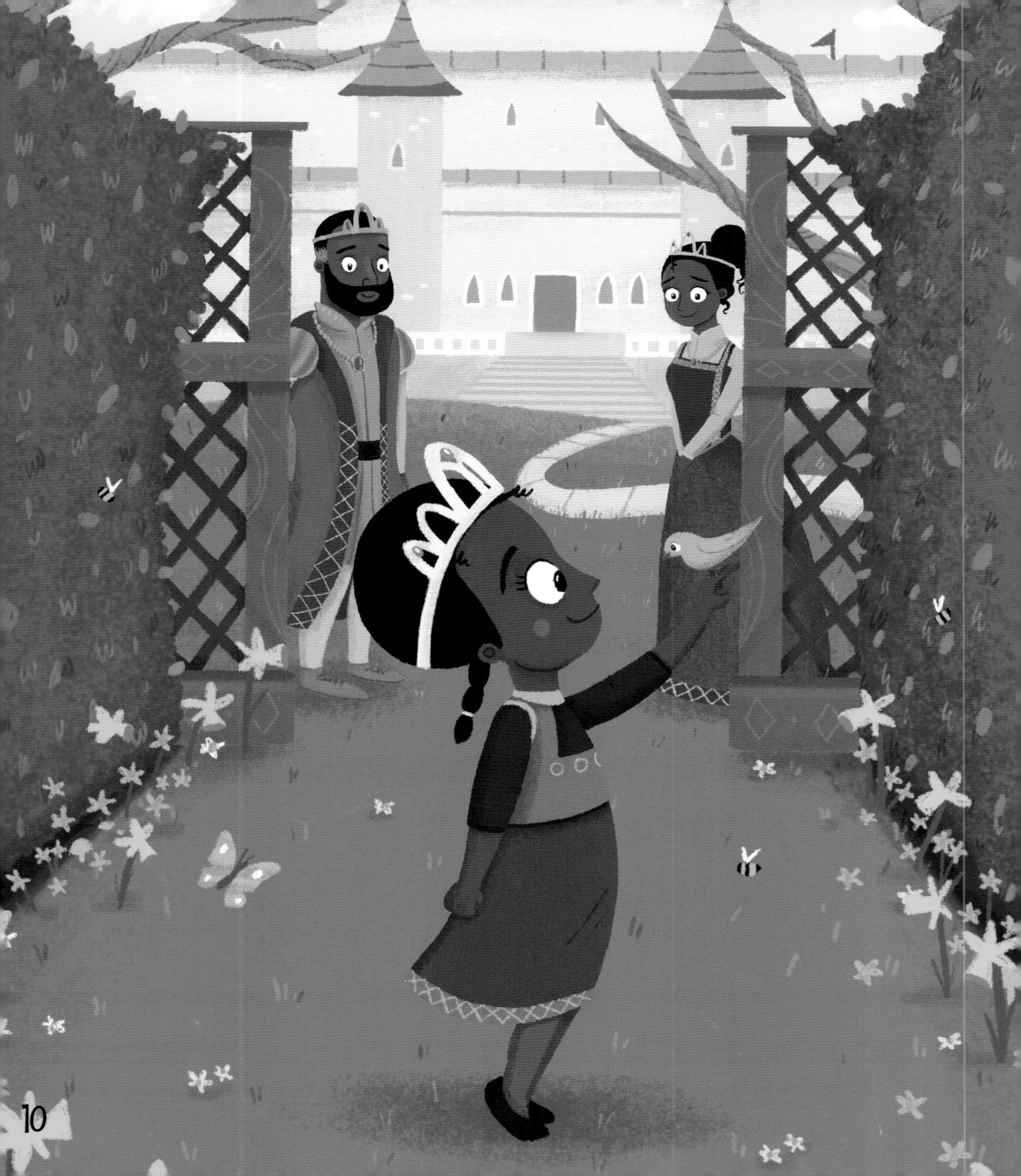

After that, the king and queen kept the princess away from pins and needles.

"Play outside," they told her. "There are no pins in the garden."

The princess loved studying the flowers and birds. She loved watching the bees and butterflies.

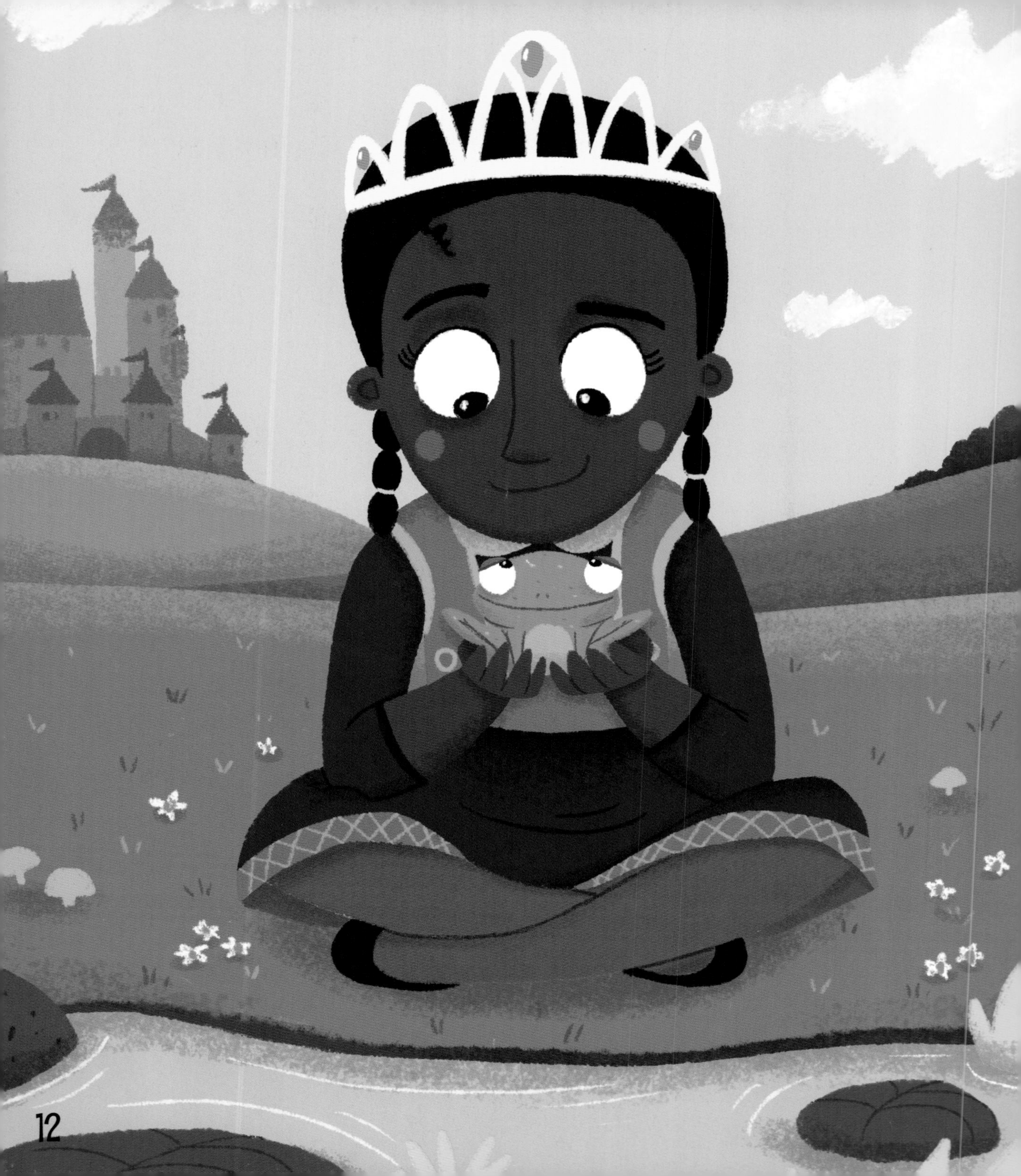

One day, just before she turned ten years old, the princess found a frog. He looked so sweet.

The princess took the frog back to the palace and put him in a tank. The frog thought she was very kind.

The princess drew a picture of the frog. But just as she was pinning it on the wall ...

MR. FROG

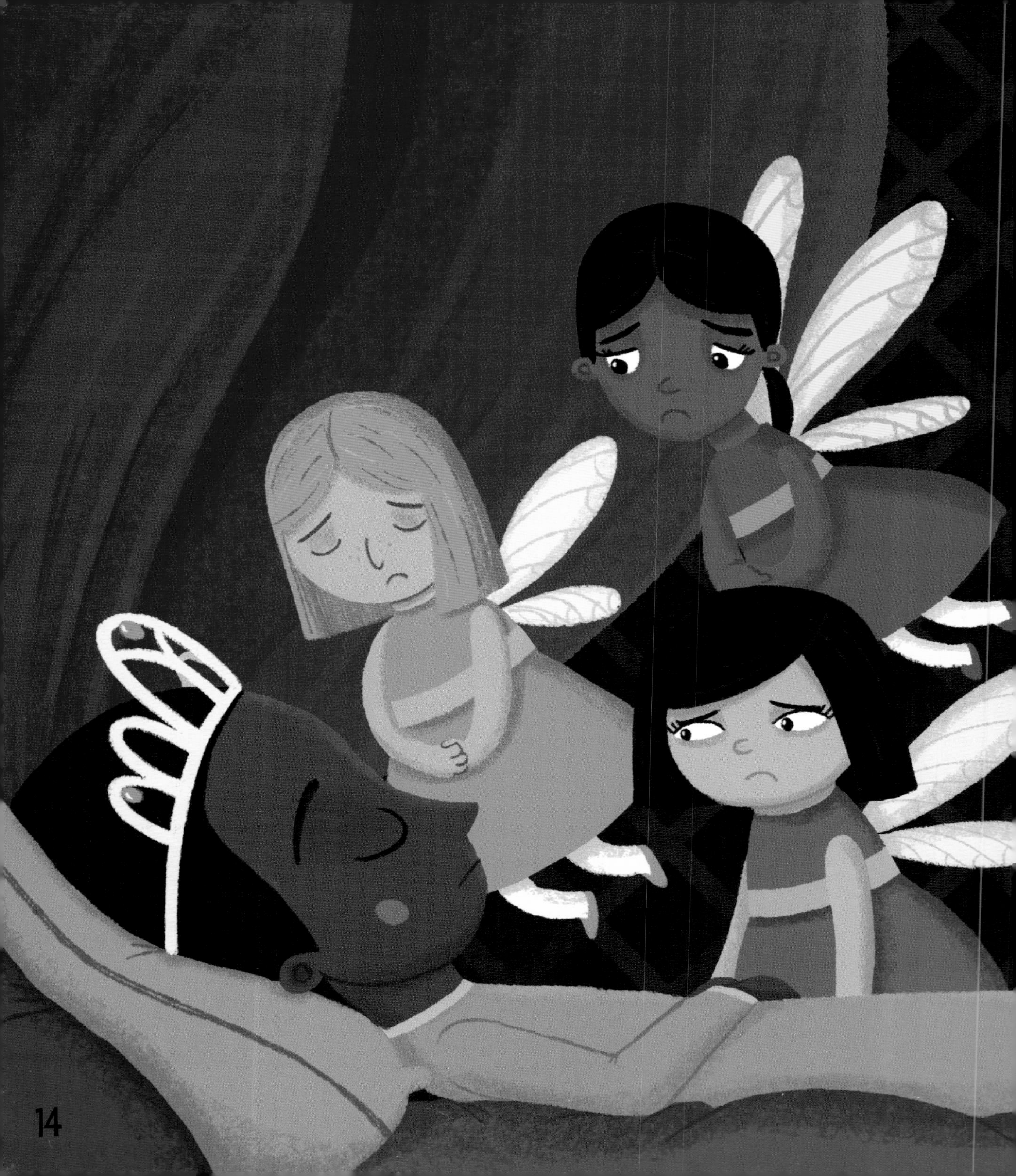

... the princess pricked her finger and fell asleep.

The *fairy* **godmothers** saw everyone in the palace was upset. They put them all to sleep, too.

"If only a prince would come and kiss her," they sighed.

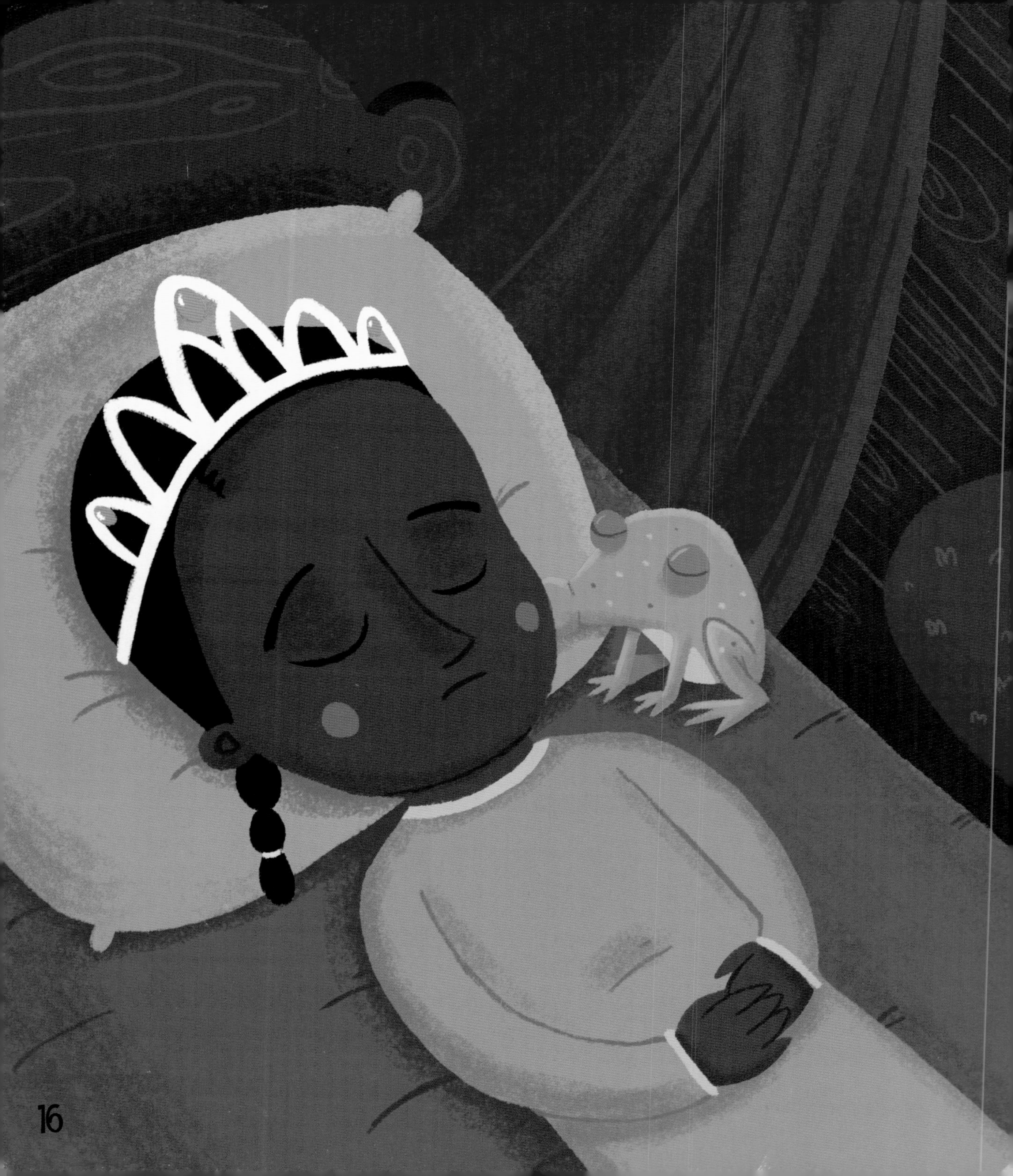

With everyone in the palace asleep, the frog was the only one left awake.

The *frog* saw that this was his chance. It was time *for* him to be a hero!

The *frog* hopped out of the tank and over to the princess's bed. Then he gave her a big, wet kiss.

When the princess woke up ...

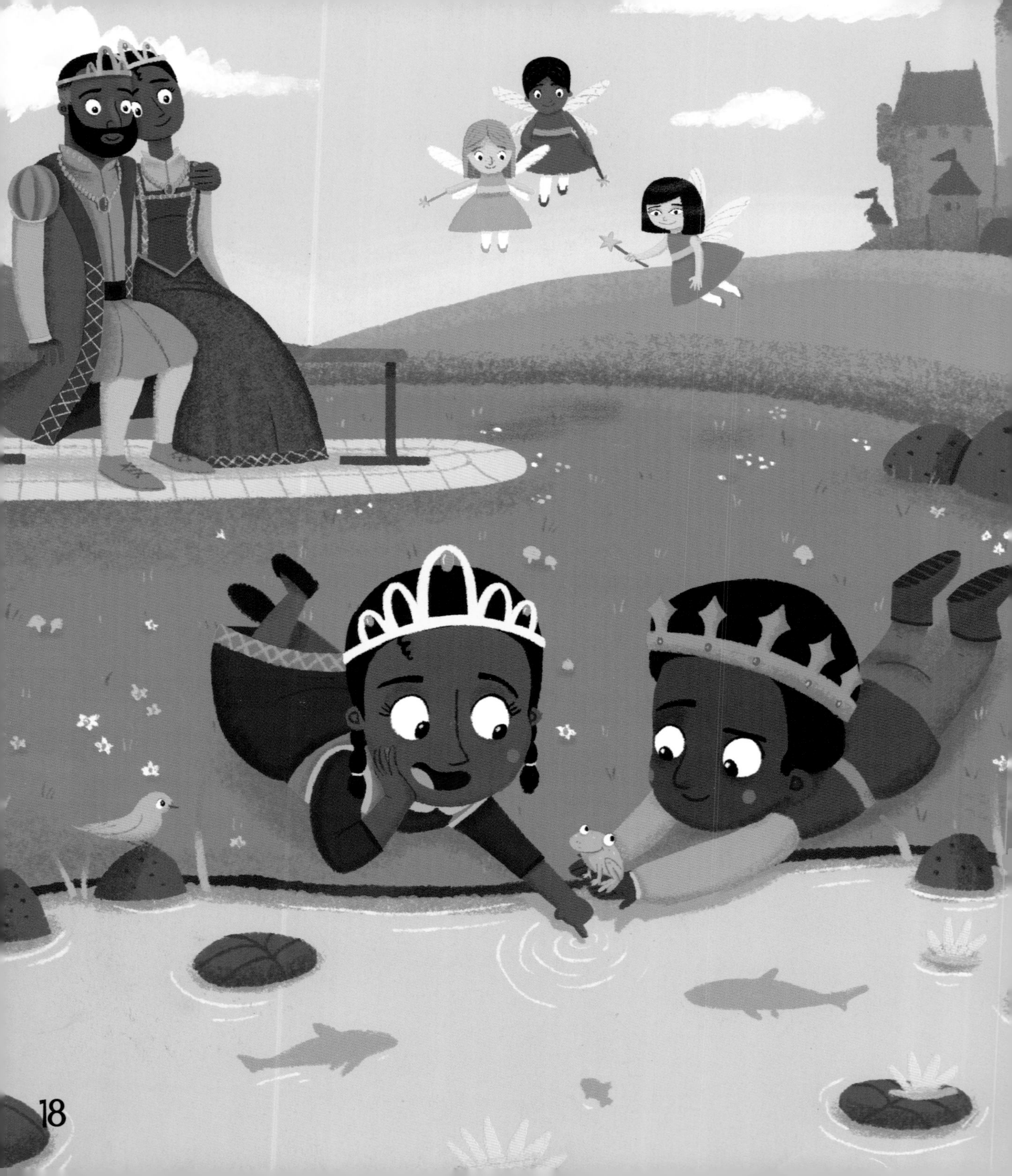

... the frog turned into a prince!

"The wicked fairy turned me into a frog," he said. "The spell could only be broken if I kissed a princess."

"Thanks for saving me!" said the princess. The fairy **godmothers** shouted for joy and woke up everyone in the palace.

The princess and the prince became best friends. Together they looked after the animals in the palace garden.

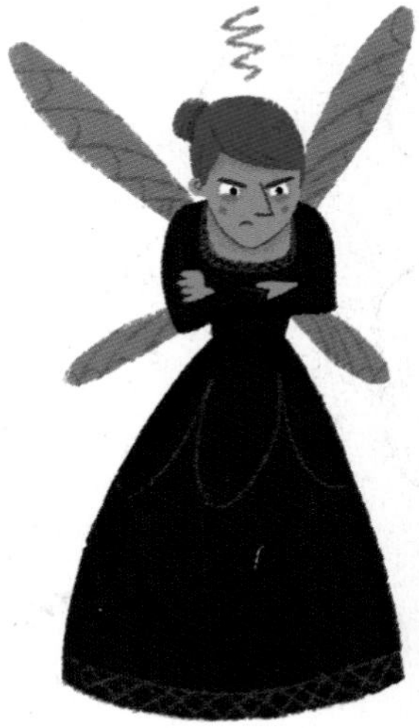

Sleeping Beauty

The story of *Sleeping Beauty* was first written down by a French writer called Charles Perrault. In the story, a king and queen have a daughter and invite seven fairy **godmothers** to her christening. A wicked fairy bursts in and puts a **curse** on the baby. She will prick her finger on a **spindle** and die. The last fairy godmother casts her own spell that the princess will not die, but will fall asleep for 100 years. Only a prince's kiss will wake her. The princess grows up, pricks her finger and falls asleep. Luckily, a prince finds the palace and wakes Sleeping Beauty.

The Frog Prince

The Frog Prince was first written down by the Brothers Grimm. They lived in Germany 200 years ago. In the story, a princess drops her golden ball into a stream and meets a frog. The princess promises that if he fetches her ball, he can live in the palace. But when he fetches her ball, she runs away. The frog goes to the palace and the king tells his daughter she must keep her word. The princess cares for the frog and, on the third day, the frog turns into a prince. He had been cursed by a wicked fairy.

Glossary

cackle – laugh in an evil way

curse – type of spell that will make bad things happen to someone

gasp – breathe in quickly in surprise

godmother – person who promises to help bring up a child in a good way

spindle – the thing which thread is wound around when someone is spinning

Writing prompts

Tell the story of what happens to the Frog Prince in his own words.

Write an invitation to the fairy godmothers asking them to come to the party.

Write a diary entry for the wicked fairy for the day of the party. How did she feel about not being invited?

Read more

Sleeping Beauty, Sally Gardner (Orion, 2011)

The Fairytale Hairdresser and Sleeping Beauty, Abie Longstaff (Corgi, 2013)

The Frog Prince, Susanna Davidson (Usborne, 2012)

The Princess and the Frog, Vera Southgate (Ladybird, 2013)

Websites

www.readwritethink.org/files/resources/interactives/fairy-tales

Visit this website to write your own mixed up fairy tale!

www.storynory.com/2005/12/16/the-sleeping-beauty

You can listen to *Sleeping Beauty* on this website.

www.twinkl.co.uk/resources/the-frog-prince/1

Download *The Frog Prince* activities on this website.

Read all the books in the series:

FAIRY TALE MIX-UPS
The Frog Prince Saves Sleeping Beauty
written by Charlotte Guillain · Illustrated by Dan Widdowson

FAIRY TALE MIX-UPS
The Elves Help Puss in Boots
written by Paul Harrison · Illustrated by Tim Sutcliffe

FAIRY TALE MIX-UPS
Three Blind Mice Team Up with the Three Little Pigs
written by Paul Harrison · Illustrated by Mariano Epelbaum

FAIRY TALE MIX-UPS
Red Riding Hood Meets the Three Bears
written by Charlotte Guillain · Illustrated by Karl West

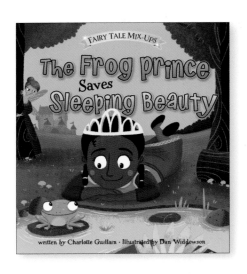

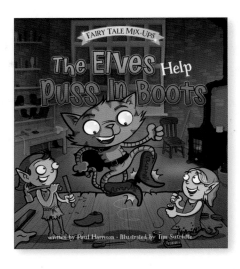

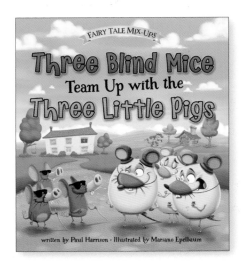

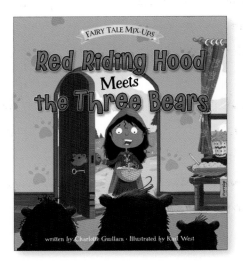

Visit www.raintree.co.uk

Raintree is an imprint of Capstone Global Library Limited, a company incorporated in England and Wales having its registered office at 264 Banbury Road, Oxford, OX2 7DY – Registered company number: 6695582

www.raintree.co.uk
myorders@raintree.co.uk

Edited by Penny West
Designed by Steve Mead
Original illustrations © Capstone Global Library Ltd 2016
Illustrated by Dan Widdowson, The Bright Agency
Production by Steve Walker
Originated by Capstone Global Library Limited
Printed and bound in China

ISBN 978 1 474 72754 9
20 19 18 17 16
10 9 8 7 6 5 4 3 2 1

British Library Cataloguing in Publication Data
A full catalogue record for this book is available from the British Library.

Every effort has been made to contact copyright holders of material reproduced in this book. Any omissions will be rectified in subsequent printings if notice is given to the publisher.

All the Internet addresses (URLs) given in this book were valid at the time of going to press. However, due to the dynamic nature of the Internet, some addresses may have changed, or sites may have changed or ceased to exist since publication. While the author and publisher regret any inconvenience this may cause readers, no responsibility for any such changes can be accepted by either the author or the publisher.